ScRuFF

ALICE BOWSHER

I wanted a dog.

This one was perfect!

No one wanted him because he looked scruffy.

But I'm a scruffy guy,
so that suited me
just fine.

Except...

and rolled

and played...

...but not Scruff.

What could be the problem?

He just loved being pampered.

So I took him for a haircut

and got mine done too.

But a simple spruce up

wasn't enough for Scruff.

And so he didn't feel left out, I washed,

brushed

and polished too.

Did we do enough?

Was Scruff still a scruff?

The competition here

was impressive.

But not as impressive as us!

SCRUFF

Written and illustrated by Alice Bowsher
Design by Mélanie Dautreppe-Liermann

British Library Cataloguing-in-Publication Data
A CIP record for this book is available from the British Library

ISBN: 978-1-908714-78-7

First published in 2020 by
Cicada Books Ltd
48 Burghley Road
London, NW5 1UE

www.cicadabooks.co.uk